# A R T E M I S
## IN ECHO PARK

Other books by the author:

*Ordinary Wisdom*
*A Packet Beating Like A Heart*
*Building Some Changes*

# ARTEMIS
## IN ECHO PARK

### POETRY
### BY ELOISE KLEIN HEALY

Firebrand
Books

Some of the poems in this collection have appeared previously in the following books or magazines: *An Ear To The Ground, The Brooklyn Review, Conditions, Contact II, Harbinger* (Los Angeles Festival and Beyond Baroque, 1990), *The High Plains Literary Review, The Jacaranda Review, The Northridge Review, Out/Look, Outweek, Poetry L/A, Poetry Loves Poetry* (Momentum Press, 1985), *Scene, Sojourner,* and *Stand Up Poetry* (Red Wind Press, 1990).

Book and cover design by Betsy Bayley
Cover photograph of Los Angeles by Marion Roth
Typesetting by Bets Ltd.

Printed on acid-free paper in the United States by McNaughton & Gunn

**Library of Congress Cataloging-in-Publication Data**

Healy, Eloise Klein.
   Artemis in Echo Park / Eloise Klein Healy.
     p.   cm.
   ISBN 0-932379-91-5 (alk. paper) — ISBN 0-932379-90-7
(pbk. : alk. paper)
    I. Title.
  PS3558.E234A7    1991
  811'.54—dc20                    91-11670
                                    CIP

# Acknowledgments

Many people have assisted me in the work of this book, and I owe them much gratitude for the encouragement and criticism delivered in the spirit of bringing these poems to completion. I am indebted to Judy Grahn and Paula Gunn Allen for their scholarly advice and generous gifts of time and attention to this project. I also want to acknowledge the contribution of Deena Metzger, specifically for her wisdom about living in the myths and mysteries. Judy Baca must certainly be thanked for drawing forth visions of the woman warrior and the moon, and Susan King for her work on Georgia O'Keeffe. I was also greatly assisted in my understanding of Artemis in all her guises by numerous writers who have done and are doing research on goddesses. The city of Los Angeles, especially my lovely Echo Park, provided a living laboratory in which to test my belief in the influence of the layers of history beneath our feet.

Special thanks go to Richard Speakes, Susan Mitchell, Patti-ann Rogers, and Lynda Hull who worked so faithfully with me on the manuscript, and to Jacqueline De Angelis who was the final arbiter of the content and a good friend of my work.

I also wish to thank the MacDowell Colony for space and time to work on the poems and to the California Arts Council for a much-needed grant.

In truth, I must credit my various animal friends who have been the best and surest guides to Artemis, especially my old dog Pauline. I regret that she did not live to celebrate this book.

Likewise, the memory of my friend May Swenson continues to shape my work, and I am thankful for her kindnesses to me.

To my parents, Ray and Carmen, and to Colleen Rooney, thank you for the help and the love.

# Contents

## Section Three

## Section Four

and beyond forgetfulness
to new remembrance

H. D., *Helen In Egypt*

There was a time when you were not
a slave, remember that. You walked alone,
full of laughter, you bathed bare-bellied.
You say you have lost all recollection of it,
remember. . . . You say there are no words
to describe this time, you say it does not
exist. But remember. Make an effort to
remember. Or, failing that, invent.

Monique Wittig, *Les Guérillères*

# SECTION ONE

# Artemis In Echo Park

I turn out the driveway, point down the street,
bend where the road bends and tip down the hill.
This is a trail, even under asphalt.
Every street downtown cuts through adobe
and the concrete wears like the curve
of a bowl baking on a patio or the sway of a brick wall
drying in the sun.
The life before cement is ghosting up
through roadways that hooves and water
have worn into existence forever.
Out to Pasadena, the freeway still behaves
like a ravine, snaking through little valleys.
The newer roads exist in air, drifting skyward,
lifting off the landscape like dreams of the future.
We've named these roads for where they end—
Harbor Freeway, Ventura Freeway, Hollywood Freeway—
but now they all end in the sky.

# The Real Bears Have Gone North

The real bears have gone north
and in their place are grizzlies,
modern noses and paws with thumbs
prowling the underbrush
of public parks and back alleys.
Once when they were sacred, the girls
went to the woods to live like bears
before becoming women. Wild for the weeks
of initiation, they slept in wooly piles
under the moon and sang the songs of bears.
Now at the grocery, wildlife roams up and down
between the cars, sniffing handouts from shoppers
and knowing better than to snap or bite.
One woman brings her own cub and maybe
the young of others. She's thin as a mongrel
and her baby's too young to hold out her own hand.
What countryside is this, what species
am I feeding with my loose change
and dollar bills, like dry leaves, I give them?
When I was a girl I had to pretend
the groves of trees were full of people.
Now the world is peopled enough
and in the middle of this tropical city
I imagine oaks, I imagine the land
could still feed us.

# Only The Moonlight Matters

What you feel in Echo Park
is population density
but only the moonlight matters.
For most of last summer
we had just lake bottom
and mud diggers collecting old bottles.
The moon came up anyway and blued out the scars
so it looked like a lake again
with waves plopping up against the rim.
We had the stabbings and such
and car thefts,
but down the hill there's a deep blue rift
darkly hollow as the first hour of sleep.
We have it all in its own round time
touched up by moonlight on schedule.
Soft music comes floating out of the houses
and what people say on the other hill
is sometimes sensible, sometimes missing part
of how the lips must meet
to press out the right sound.

# Now I Find My House Is Not Safe

Now I find my house is not safe
from my desires.
A woman comes to my door
a week early for our appointment.
How surprised I am
to want her without preliminaries.
This is the strange price of my solitude,
always on the edge
of taking whatever path leads away
from the deep pond that's been the center
of my world for months.
But a howl in the woods
and my quick dogs of feeling
rise up and circle.
They know I'm already moving
and want to move.

# Public Water

I buy Arrowhead and have forgotten
what public water tastes like.
The city periodically sends out
the recipe it's using,
but it's not like reading
the names of streams
and their linkages to rivers.
I like the word *tributary* for its taste
and a *stream* is something I practice
as a state of feeling,
or I imagine that one used to cut through
the place where my garage sits
down at the bottom of my hill.
I believe in the ghosts of streams
as much as I love my memory of Green River
and its town we passed through
on trips to the Midwest.
The area wasn't particularly scenic
but the river was wide
and looked good to drink.
At the drugstore next to the movie theatre
in my hometown I drank Coca-Cola with lime syrup
and we called it a Green River.

# The Valley Of The Amazons

She went to the grocery store with me
in North Hollywood wearing a black tank top
and no bra. We stood together in line.
Everybody was looking at her breasts,
her aviator glasses, her hair slicked back
and one strand falling over her eyes.
I felt like we were in a clearing
ready to mount the horses.
The men stood at a distance.
Our nakedness was nonchalant, connected
to horses and skin warmth. We would ride off
when the checker tallied our purchases
and the clearing would smell like horses
the rest of the day.

# I Live Where I Live

I live where I live because
it has nothing to do with me.
I could go on about the choices I've made
and all the other elements of my landscape
emotionally carved or artfully decorated,
but the real truth is, here you can see
the ribs showing through.
The land's way eventually surfaces.
It's all softening like old chenille,
faint voices on patios in the summer nights.
So I say this has nothing to do with me
but it comes to my door
and I let it in. I have the conversation
I wouldn't have with Jehovah's Witnesses.
I have brandy. I cook a little red snapper.
I remember Mazatlán and the plants
taking over, turning over the pots,
covering walls. This has nothing to do with me,
this wildness that softens everything.
Then again, it has nothing to do but me.

# This Is Not Really A House At All

This is not really a house at all.
The wind simply changes direction here.
Even the papers on my table
have no sacred order.
I find them out of sorts and lost
from my purposes in the corners
or fluttering, captivated by the wind
and wanting to go where it's going.
They have no loyalty to my house
now that they know the truth.
This is not really a house at all
in the weather of my life.

# The City Beneath The City

I own a print of cows on a green hill,
brown-and-white cows
like peaceful wooden cutouts
who dream me through the wall,
through my neighbor's house, straight back
to old Pasadena—Rancho San Pasqual,
Rancho Santa Anita, and the wild cows
with arching horns, their spines knobbed
and hairy, 3-D and mean.

Their hides, I know, became chairs a century ago,
the hair reddish brown and white wore smooth.
The extra hides shipped down to the harbor
were traded for furniture carted home
to the main house on the two-wheeled *carettas*
up the track that's now the Harbor Freeway
out the ravine to Pasadena.

Little black olives pocking the dust
were picked and pickled in brine.
In the *zanjas*, horses drank
and scum floated on the water
green as neon.
From los ranchos to Sonora,
young ladies traveled in society.
The population of Chinese workers
was kept small—no women allowed—but
under the Governor's mansion, while
his daughter gave piano recitals and sang,
the Chinese dug tunnels north
from Olvera Street where their wives would live
in hiding. Under the cover of night
they spread out the secret earth to dry.

Some days still the ground shivers, splits
open the face of an unmined seam.
The city beneath the city dances
like a *calavera* in the ballroom of the dead.
The old bones shake when a shovel
strikes an amber bottle
or excavations uncover stone canals
mysterious as the mountains on the moon.

# Toltecs

Radio about a foot-and-a-half
wide swinging at his side.
Three boys abreast and one
has the radio playing loud rock
they talk to as they walk
past my house. Three boys
dressed in their style
of short jackets and caps pulled
down almost to their eyes.
They might as well be naked
boys in the hot sun singing
in a changing boy voice the songs
they like to hear. They might
as well be boys chipping rocks
into weapons or tools.
But they are only boys on the way
someplace. They have to be men
sometime and no time for idle
rambling to rock music unless
they take jobs in the outdoors
where they can still be boys
and dress to get dirty. They can
be boys underneath the culture
forever because some other man
will gladly take those boys
and chip them down into tools
or weapons or bake them into
the walls of his own idea
of empire.

# The Peahens

River noise replacements have appeared.
Massive rumble of the freeway
in the afternoon. Truck going down
through its gears. Helicopter cutting a circle.
Across the street the black-and-white dotted
dog some call Daisy or Droopy or Bonnie
looks like a cow grazing on the steep lawn.
That's where the peahens stood so still
the day one of them walked in front
of a car. Her wings hushed in air
and whacked on the pavement
and a thick red river of blood pooled
like red tar on the asphalt.
Her sisters stood like frightened girls
or stone statues. They ignored the wake
of bread bits and birdseed I set out.
They didn't venture onto the street
much after that. Then someone shot one
from its perch. One was stolen. One's left.
I hear her calling over the rush of wind
in the avocado tree.

# This Is A Year To Keep And Give Away

This is a year to keep and give away.
I am deciding the smallest things
like stones at the bottom of a stream.
I am deciding mud nests for swallows
will stay where the birds have daubed them.
The mockingbird will stay in the cypress
and translate that tree each morning.
The bamboo will stay because the Korean woman
kissed it and told me its name.
This is the year to give away, give away
what won't teach me on its own terms.
What will stay will stay for its voice.

# The Introductions

1

He is my daddy
and I am going up in his arms.
The coat he wears is gruff
and I am a puffy baby
in a snowsuit, my new suit.

There is a blur of light
and scary spin as I rise
along the trunks of his legs,
in the branches of his arms,
to the cliff of his chest.

My daddy, I am turning from him
to find my others in the circle.
When I turn again, his face
scratches my cheek. My mother
is crying, "That's your daddy,"
the thick green Army coat
who has lifted me, who is holding me,
who has glasses like my mother
and the little circles of light
shine back at me.

He is ours,
they say, he is mine.
My daddy.

## 2

That light in the stairwell,
I could see it from my crib.

It was alone with me, sometimes
at my feet, sometimes rising
up over my arm as I turned.
What I learned first before speech
was close and far
in the form
of light.

How close? How far?
Every grown-up day that's the question.
Alone sometimes, sometimes turning
to another, that old feeling
I can't talk about.

How close. How far.

## 3

In my family, nobody talks
about what's outside the circle.
What's inside has been decided secretly
and an animal is born in me
when I try to confide my feelings.

Its chest heaves with a human sound,
a nervous cough at what might be
found out and how close it is
to speech.

Soon I will say something
my father will have to hear.
He will feel a blow to his chest.
He will blink his eyes at me,
disbelieving.

Someone should have prepared him
as they prepared me—*she's your baby.*


4

All these friends of mine,
these unmarried women
my father wonders about.
I'm always surprised he doesn't know
their names after all these years.
Nor does he know them
as lovers—mine and each other's.
Nor the way these shades of feeling shift
and create family circles,
traveling bands.

Sometimes I imagine us on the frozen tundra,
a place like Lapland, and we are bundled
in our tribal gear, pushing through
the eternal winters of our years.

I will tell him about this life of mine,
the scenes along the way,
and how I am among my kind
a shuffling she-bear,
trail-crashing omnivore
looking for a fat trout,
a sweet of berries,
a deep warm pocket to put my coat in
for a long season.

# SECTION TWO

# Artemis

I am thinking about romance and its purpose.
Children and why I didn't have any.
I would have left the cave and them with it
or I would have tied them to me forever
with my own sad dreams and finicky order.

I've liked young animals better.
I could put their heads in my mouth.
I could lick and clean them like a mother,
but I could not raise a child.
The first thing a child should see
is the pink sunrise of a nipple, not the green wind
of a branch whipping in passing.

I chose to keep animals around me instead
because we are the same. We have habits
and make strange circles before we sleep.
We don't like to be watched while we eat.

# Seeing Agnes Varda's *The Vagabond*

1

Sitting in the dark
I am remembering
that I have lost a woman
while a woman is losing herself
in front of me.

The scenes spill out
like what has already happened.
I can't keep anything straight:
bursts of weather, her body in her clothes,
the sibilance in her voice.

First the young woman's a corpse
in a ditch, then she's like Venus
walking naked out of the water
with the voice-over saying
*I believe she came out of the sea.*

Was she twisting her hair?
Was she leaning over slightly
to twist her long hair?
Did she do anything to modulate
the arrogance in her walk,
the arrogance of that black pubic patch,
full thighs, her heavy-breasted
plunge into the world?

## 2

I have dealt out these images for days,
laid out the scenes
like forks and knives and plates.
Sat myself down at the table
to devour her, her goat cheese, a tough
chunk of bread. End the meal with
a cadged cigarette and smoke a joint
later. Share a bottle of wine, her
camp bed.

## 3

I don't question what the film means.
I, too, have lost something.
I feel the dust in the room
from the plaster falling,
remember the word *radish*
as she said it
and can feel her
pulling on wet clothes,
feel how a cold zipper
is fatigue itself.

I just want to know
when her journey started,
not why she left.
And another young woman,
framed and stuck
sitting at a table
with her silent father
repeating one word—*freedom, freedom.*

Why did she stay?

# Hawks

You have to come to this house
on purpose.
It's not on a street to take
instead of another street.
It's more a series of soft turns
down a slope.
No hard edges.

The last house I lived in
got me here.
It was the first time I'd lived
off the ground.
My street looped like a lazy belt
around the waist of a hill
near the stars.

And higher up, two hawks perched
above a raw little valley.
The first day I saw them
the air was umber.
It was almost night.

A hunting pair
twenty feet from the roadway
exposed on two bare tree limbs.
The female turned to face me
and tore my sight open
without a stroke.
She split the urban fabric instantly.
Hawk talon,
farming small animals
on a grassy slope.

# Another Island

The old man sleeps on the little lawn
of the Korean Rosicrucian Church.
He positions himself like a cardboard cutout
all over Echo Park, sometimes by the curb
at Safeway, sometimes staring there
into the traffic as if it were a stream.
He always wears the same trimmed beard
and eyes like cloudy mornings.

Wherever he went with his youth
he didn't come home.
He hunkers down on his heels and sings,
brown bottle neck the instrument of his song.
He sits on the curb
and waves cover his ankles.

Even if I should catch his eye,
I couldn't find him.
I have a different island
to attend to and I don't try to stop
the spinning door between the worlds.
I remember very carefully
how to come back.

# Patterns

When I was a freshman in college we all herded
into the auditorium to take the MMPI. *Do you
have a tight band around your head? Are you afraid
of doorknobs? Do you like mannish women?*
A pattern emerged. My friend from high school
marked she liked mannish women. I wondered what
pattern would emerge of me and I aimed for the top
two percent. We were invited to make an appointment.
We were invited to discuss. I let myself flatten
into my file. I liked Amy Lowell's *Patterns*.
The squills and daffodils. The garden path.
I wrote a poem about buttons like gold sea anemones,
the sea purple as a wine-dark tunic against my cheek.
I did not discuss what I felt at an appointment.

# This Place Named For Califia

If the sun weren't just now setting,
or maybe it's the mist—
this season's late night and early
morning fog—you could see it
off the coast, simple as Catalina
but bejeweled as a barge on the Nile,
that island, floating like the legends
ahead of an exploring army.
The story of the women beyond
the river, the falls, or like this
place, the island of women
in this place, black Amazons
living without men just beyond
the mist, beyond this weather. Dazzling
as it rises, an island real enough
to be necessary, a kind of woman
necessary enough to be real.

# Up To Topanga

Up to Topanga the road cuts down
to the muscle, a sea-laid matrix
of rock and shell the creek carves through.
Full moon, the sea at my back
glazed dark blue.
There's a coyote in my headlights
with her inevitable smile.
Sweet dancer, she leaps the double line
and I climb higher, following your car.
The man who tried to pick you up
at dinner started a war in me.
I could have charged with furious tusks
in that underbrush of talk, but I kept it
where women like me keep things, quiet—
until later when you held me like a girl.
Eyes smiling like coyote, you changed
my jealousy into passion, threw your hair
over me like a coat of fur, and into the forest
of the moon I chased you.

# The Path Back To The Heart

Her body closing around me
like a maze,
which strand suffices
as the path back to the heart?
My hands are slippery
following her,
weaving into the tendrils
sweated along her neck.
Words fall from her mouth
like hot entrails
when skinning out a deer.
Fallen, we're both fainting
in the body's steam, in the blood
pushing, parching me
as I sing
a syllable behind her cry.

# Roofs

Roofs. Now which color wins?
Red shows best, but if I wait
then there are many green ones
and mine is the newest.
Mine is new but plain.
The old green one down the hill
is laid on with a scallop design
so it looks like a fishnet
or mossy old carp.
Another one, maybe its garage,
swims alongside, pointed upstream
toward Silverlake Reservoir.
When I think about it,
my house is on the bank
and not swimming away.
You could tie a boat to my cypress.
You could think you were in a painting
in this light, this time of day,
ready to fish.

# Another Poet Writes About Love

Another poet writes about love
and I'm puzzled.

It's out there for him
in what he calls a lady.

He says she touches him
lightly on the ribs,

but I'm sure it's just his idea
that's touched. Something's missing

in his conception of completion.
He wants her to bring it to him,

be Eve at nightfall coming home,
completing him with tenderness.

I have been with women enough to want
tenderness igniting, sending the ribs

out to their filled extension
and sparks of flame

down the dry tendrils of my arms.
I want to die and rise and never be

completed in tenderness.
I want to burn the covering plants

to the ground and mulch them under.
I want good black earth instead of love.

# The Girl

I don't know the children in the next block
but the ones I saw on my walk played like strangers.
Their clothes were new and clean and they watched
each other's eyes to see what to do next.
She was the oldest one and thin. She twirled
her hands. They rose and fell like leaves.
The little boys ran in a ring around her
and once around the tree. Who knows what they were singing.
Once around the block and my dog and another dog
growled and snapped and drew blood. Once around the block
and the boys were still running in their ring.
I saw her this time as a tall girl, her head
already above the first branches of the small tree.
The boys were merely children.

# Advice Like That

The woman had the boy by the hand.
He was maybe nine years old. He was dirty.
His mouth was smeared and his stomach stuck out
where his shirt ended and his pants began.
She had on a cloth coat. We all had that kind
in the '60s like Jackie Kennedy. A nappy texture,
but this one sagged from its shoulders, her shoulders.

She held the boy out to me and said could I give
her something so she and her baby
could have breakfast.
I gave her a dollar. She smiled. No teeth on the right side.
She looked me up and down. *Honey,* she said,
*them wind things blowing in the road,*
*don't walk through them no more.*

She and the boy went to Burrito King.
I drove out to the Valley to my therapist.
A dollar is little to spend for advice like that.

# Georgia

I see the film about Georgia O'Keeffe
once a semester
and watched Susan's book *Georgia*
as she wrote it and printed it.

Lightning through a skull.
Susan knew it, too. White bone of a cow, white
bone where the light strikes color.
That's how it works.

If O'Keeffe hadn't lived in Abiquiu
she could easily have perched
in the last house up near Elysian Park,
right down from the hawks.

The lay of that land
needs a fierce tenant. The edge
of a mesa, a skyscraper, a wave.

# Behind The Garden

She lived in that cool room
behind the garden.
She had a habit of brushing her cheek
with her finger.
I started doing it, a branch brushing
against my face
as if I were going somewhere
through trees.

I left everybody at the beach
just to sit with her in her yard.
I read the same page of Harold Bloom
over and over again.
She had her shirt off.
When I asked about it, she denied
any connection between us.
Cups of tea she said she didn't pour.

It was just about noon when I left.
As I swung up the freeway ramp and down again,
the city was frighteningly clear.
She said she said nothing to me. And she said,
*Don't come back. You've made a stupid mistake.*
*You're worthless.*

In her yard, I'd looked at
my tennis shoes, traced and traced
the laces. She said
she said nothing to me.

# Cactus

In the nursery, I always go to the cactus first.
Who are they anyway? Old ghosts, perhaps,
who meet you on their own terms.
Then I leave them and walk into ferns, cooler
heads, and palms, long arms and secretive.
I circle. If this were love I'd be thinking
*opposites attract* because I'm back
at the cactus counter fixed on someone
called Goat's Head. But what did that poet say,

the one who was holding a woman so high
off the ground? Something about tenderness in love?
When I look at the cactus in my hand,
my hand carefully raising the green plastic cup,
I think love is the spines,
the spines that curve and radiate
in parallel lines.
Love is how close you can get and even bleed
and even want to pick it up again.

# Wisteria

This pale winter the wisteria looks like an empty
nest. When I look deeper, there is an empty nest
inside her. The reason the mockingbird kept flying in.
I have to do some talking with this plant. In the summer
it's such an argument I just stay away. She wants
to be playful and slap my arms when I trim her.
She's like a twelve-year-old girl, and she stings me with
the venom in her leaves. Now is the only time
I can handle her. Asleep and slow, she's just a brown plan
which will become complicated again.
I'll have a good talk with her while she dozes.
Convince her she's simply a wild girl, that what she needs
is a good haircut, a fresh outlook, another chance
to really show her stuff.

# Ceremony

*for Barbara Myerhoff*

At the ceremony for Barbara's death, there was a garment
for each of us. Layers of the world floated and changed
positions. The colors of dark berries warmed the room.
Green leaves—shining, and waxy, and perfumed—arched
above the table. Death not there. Life not there as struggle.
Red berries and the immense night transparent as a jewel.
We were not bereft in our ceremony for the woman
we count now as one of our dead. Green forms, the shock of
clear color beat like a pulse. All night we sang and chanted,
swaying like branches and praying like trees covered with
winter berries, heavy with fruit in a strange season.

# SECTION THREE

# Springtime

Springtime, I thought how nice
to see all the babies at the zoo.
My eleventh-grade girls gathered
to watch the bears fuck
and the giraffes try to.

I thought how nice to see some cubs,
but then the zoo was filled with children
and among the hundreds
two of them on leashes, staring
the way a puppy and a kitten
will stand and stare and try to lick.

There were box turtles in a pond, floating
like seeds on the water,
climbing with their bear claws up onto a log
like moons in a slow rising cycle.

Turtles that taste like seven other meats,
but I couldn't eat them now, or the ranch-grown
rabbits in the grocery, slick in shrink-wrap.
No blue pocking where the shot stayed lodged
in the rabbits my dad brought home dead.

But I can't leave the turtles—
the old rattle of medicine shells,
the flash of red lightning and yellow lightning
on their necks, the caves they enter
and the vault of bone they dream in.

Once at the airport in a case, I saw lacquered turtle backs
and a sign propped up on a snakeskin purse,
*Don't buy these products!*

# She Claims She Does Not Know

*I don't know anything about Artemis,* she said
in her letter. My friend who lives with a wolf
on a mountaintop. Who is keening over a man.
The point of her heart is lodged in that wood
and so she does not know. In the dead of winter
her friend will die, not the man, but the friend
she shares a soul with. The wolf who sleeps under
the table will break out of the house because
he is in love. My friend will write a book
about her own name and break a dry stick off
at the point of her heart. But she claims
she does not know.

# Some Love Stories

I'm not in love but I am alive.
When the man in the story I was reading
talked about love I had trouble looking back.
Mainly I was reminded of the way
I have sat on patios with women
I was in love with.
The feeling I remember most
was wanting to go back in the house.
I'm certain the author didn't anticipate
such a response though he had lots of
living room furniture in his story
and nobody moving.
It was like one long back rub
with no sexual overtones.
I have often had to give them
but don't like the dead-end feeling
of relaxing somebody into inactivity.
Maybe this is love in the way I don't like it.

# Chinois

Across the room at Chinois Joan Didion was having lunch
with her husband. The little mushrooms on my plate
were almost too beautiful to eat so I looked at her
and watched her drink white wine. I wanted
her autograph. I wanted to crawl on my knees to her
table but thought better of it. The food was expensive.
She would not want to be bothered and I should have
been eating what I ordered before it cooled off. Anyway,
I was having a conversation that was serious and painful.
The waiter was overly polite and my companion overly
demanding. Or was it just the hot wind from the north?
Joan Didion would have understood that. I started
with the mushrooms and the fine crackling skin of the
duck.

# What It Was Like The Night Cary Grant Died

Cary Grant was dying all that time
we took to talk about romance
and what little chance there is
to see on screen even the evening we spent,
talk and turn of events, how everything went
this way for the dyke singer and that
for the queer star, and what a funny
type we are, so normal in our taste
for bliss, but then there's the way
we kiss, unseemly on the screen
to see so much between two women,
the queen card played upon the queen.

And Cary Grant was dying until dawn
the night we carried on and on
about romance, the chances in a glance,
the votes we cast for whom we've asked
into our hearts' open beds. What was it
Dietrich said? No more talkative alive
than dead, that one, and who's to blame
for her closed case, the gorgeous face
that couldn't change its straight facade.
It would have been too odd to see
a woman in a pair of pants begin
her dapper dandy dance. An audience
would have died from it—the fragile pair,
the dalliance, the slicked-back hair.

The King of Romance drifted off from Iowa
and Hollywood the night he was to say
what it was like for him. The night he died,
that night we came away from talking until dawn
about the scenes and sounds that don't go on
the screen in living color of what's between
a woman lover and her lover.

# The Amazons

You haven't been to a dance
that didn't have its Amazons,

or any salon, or any new world
they didn't already inhabit,

or stream they didn't ford,
or man they didn't lord.

Oh, the power of myth, it's said,
the psychological projection of the Greeks!

But you haven't been to a dance
the Amazons didn't dance

or held a woman
who hasn't wondered.

# The Shape Of Female Desire

A lecturer once asked,
    what does the shape
    of female desire look like on stage,
    or for that matter, women talking to one another?

And she said,
    the performance space,
    could it assume
    something other than the traditional shape?

I would answer with the face of the stripper
at the birthday party when she saw
the room was filled with women.

and what I said to you,
    let's not go see.

We sat on the patio instead,
dressed in leather jackets
zipped to our chins.
Someone passed you a cigarette.
I touched the arm of your jacket, a new one
bought the year we weren't together.
A long time with two winters in it.

The party was a surprise
for a woman we didn't know.
The night was cold as a sapphire
and our breaths wove a blue mist in it,
that shape in and out of us—wanting again.

# Changing The Oil

I get her up on the curb, two wheels off the street
and dive under with my tools—my favorite blue-handled
wrench and a drop-forged hammer with a no-slip grip.

Her, her, her—always the female car. And now I'm under,
lying on the news of the day before yesterday, slowly turning
the warm nut. She's above me like a womb or heaven
about to rain. I'm slowly turning my way into her
black blood, slipping on the wet bolt, diving into
the underworld we women crawl into with our new pride
fresh from the parts store. Turning the beautiful
implements over in my hands, tenderly
the oil spurts free—and I have done it.

# Like A Wick, I Thought

Like a wick, I thought, a woman.
No, she was like smoke from a candle.
She was not burning, but smoke like the shred
that hangs when the fire is pinched out.
There with her shopping cart at Sunset
and North Spring, grey as the dusky November
night, at third glance she could have been
a man, bearded and gaunt. A winter pelt of hair.
Who can tell? Something hormonal gone
beyond repair. Like the grocery lot lady
who's grown a goatee. She sings and strokes
it and croons with her head tipped back.
Some star or moon has captured her song.
She sings up at it through the smoky sky,
a greybeard now, a wisp of wisdom song
and a cigarette she waves through the air
like a wand.

# The Singing

One who came home from the moon singing,
they hid him. They gave him rest
from "stress" and kept him off TV
with his stories of his body
filled with someone starry.
The black loop around the back
and the singing that filled him
threw him at the feet of the spirit.

He came back without the Book.
There will be no beginning
in the Word.
It will be instead the turtle
of light, the rabbit of the tongue
ululating like the women in the meadow
at the Music Festival
the day I finally understood why men fear us—
four thousand naked female voices
bursting out of their tarps and rain gear
and the moon rising up through the rainbow.

# Moon On The Porch

Moon on the porch thumps his tail when I climb
the stairs. He's got a rock in his mouth, old dog,
and will I play? Old teeth worn into stubs
from carrying rocks. Old Moon who limps
as far as we'll walk him. Drinks from the hot
tub when you're not looking, when the moon slides
over the edge of the roof and naked into the water.
I didn't know then this would be a poem to all
my lovers, planted by you in the full moon,
the water running off your breasts, falling
like silver coins into a pool. I didn't know then
how many women I was learning to love.

# Going Down To The Sunless Sea

An editorial appeared in the *Times*
by a homeless man about a homeless woman
who had glittering eyes and no shoes.
In the '60s we would have seen her
in her naked rags and said, *far out!*

She isn't out.
The gods appear at the fringes
just where the grip is about to give way.
That's what Jesus meant
about the least among us
and why he went to the desert.

The fringe from her side
has simply overlapped with this one's wilderness
and she is standing by the stream
that runs between them.
What we see reflected in her eyes
is that river.
It has had many names in its time.
It even ran through Los Angeles underground,
slaked the sandy arroyos and sank,
percolating into the clay.
She can stand on a concrete curb and hear it
running through her and out onto the street,
up and over the opposite curb.

How many names has it had?
Running down to a sunless sea
I think is how I remember it described best.

# SECTION FOUR

# The Concepts Of Integrity And Closure
# In Poetry As I Believe They Relate To Sappho

1

There's always the question
*what else?* or *what more?*
A fragment of papyrus,
a frame from a film.
Wholeness but no closure.
Just what you'd glimpse—
two women suddenly arm in arm
crossing the beach-front walk,
the waves running like mares
behind them.


2

What is a month, for example?
Tear it out of a year like an eye
and what do you see?
Unimaginable to expect a year
could be missing an eye, or is it harder
to think of it
having one? Questions of parts
of what,
this is how I've felt
trying to look out of my self.
Just quick takes,
motor-driven and waiting for the day
it all makes sense.

3

Sappho is the lesson of parts.
Libraries you must do without
because you are the book.

4

This is what happens at parties
where women dance with one another.
Everyone kisses. Old lovers.
Tribes assume this.
Kiss and kiss. Just that much of that.
Book and book and book. I have been learned
by heart. Lovely Sappho taking in
a glance at a lovely thigh, flower
arranging someone's hair.
Like that.

Across the patio
in a canvas chair, you know
the living danger sitting there.
A fragmentary glance. An hour
in her arms, disarray
you carry for another hour
or a year, years from that day
you keep like a piece of mica or a negative.

I have held to my lips
for a moment things like smoke. Smoke
from a burning book.

5

The waves ran away like mares
and the silver sat in its soft cloth
and the shells of the sea rolled
and dragged lovingly up and back.
And some of those women simply saw
each other and some of them saw
the sea.

But Sappho, she saw everything.

# Cactus Girls

They spread up hillsides
looking like coral reefs.
Green flat fans taking over
a south-facing slope,
then thick red pipes of fruit—
sticky, overflowing, sweet.

I've had long friendships
with those girls but
don't like cactus candy
or love that flows sweet
only through the menace of argument,
thorny and complex.
I like the sweet pink trumpet flowers
that bloom overnight
and then are gone.
I can taste that pink
all the year it takes to bloom again.

One night a star-shaped tube blossomed.
It was a full moon
and the patio was as bright as a room.
The blossom actually grew wide in front of me,
skin-colored and flecked with dots of purple
leading deep into its heart where another star,
a white one, stretched out.

Maybe it was all a dream, but in the morning
the flower hung there like a spent kite,
a sweet and worthwhile death,
but so much like skin
I sometimes want to peel it off the surface
of my memory.

# Snakes

Just one muscle,
the snake in the garden was striped
black and yellow, but that was in another place,
not here where snakeskin
looks like sandy pebbled arroyos,
the same color as air.
This snake is every which way a flexion, a moving
texture on the ground, speckled as a new road
with its first peppering of oil.

The rattlers migrating down to the valley floor
made a freeway past my cabin, used the side
entrance where the screen was loose
to crawl under my house
before their plunge down the short notch
to Bumblebee Canyon.
I could see them from my porch
as they left, their fresh loops
stretching forward, their wise tongues
tasting for danger.

I let them have everything—the hillsides,
the bushes—and kept to my own trail,
the driveway. I felt safe enough
not walking into the brush
but dreamed each night of snakes,
sometimes in bunches
like strands of muscle.
I was never free
of the hiss of muscle and fear
up the backs of my legs.

# From Space

Photos from space, the pretty ones anyway,
are computer generated
and look a lot like cartographers' renderings
of the New World
before explorers arrived at it.

I prefer the grimy black-and-white snapshots
inside the ships, the shuttle crew asleep
and their arms drifting overhead
like hieratic statues,

their arms escaping the sleeping sacks
like serpents crawling from their eggs,
grain sprouting from seed.
White arms and black arms and now
breasts, too, free from gravity.

# Stranded

My rear wheel yanked off
from the van
and stranded me
on the downside shoulder
of the freeway entrance lane.
Cars coming like a pack
of flat-headed dogs after game.
They were blind to me
and I was lame, locked there
high on the grinding shore,
more noise than I'd ever
heard before from waves
or storms, and around my feet
perfect stars of windshield glass
and tail lights, glinting
metal in crazy twists.
I'm an alien here
in my flesh, traveler
untethered from
the mother ship, adrift
in a cloud of space-junk
which through a window
at a safe speed
looks like harmless matter,
no longer useful,
just dead.

# Moroni On The Mormon Temple/
# Angel On The Wall

Moroni is a foreigner
and not one of the angels living here.

He was imported to point at heaven.
His name is hard and final,

not like Angel, soft *n* and soft *g*
whose name is sprayed down the street

eye-level, arm-level on a building,
quick and at night

to say, *I am no foreigner,*
*this is my barrio,*
*something old, something here.*

# Two Centuries In One Day

The couple painted on the Bridal Shop
on Broadway are six-stories high
and done up in a bright blue wash.
I like to think they're in the nineteenth century
and feeling close to the ground.
The twentieth century wants to get off the planet
but you'd never know it
from the traffic on this street.
*Titulos en Español. Discos Latinos.*
Soft tacos with shredded beef.
This is Alta California,
land of the tomato, apple of love.

The couple looms above and can look
into the offices of the *Los Angeles Times.*
Their wedding reception swirls
on the street below, and in the parking lot
one hundred years ago today
the horses doze in the sunlight.

In this sunlight it's all a wedding today,
never mind the century.

# From Los Angeles Looking South

Orderly traffic, a normal day
and 350,000 Salvadorians are in hiding
in Los Angeles.
Four women sit on the patio of El Rescate,
dirt packed hard from use.

Lydia's the weaver of this story
and two local women translate the Spanish,
pull the threads straight for me.

She has given this testimony for others
besides me. She's slight, simply dressed,
a former philosophy student, a suspect.

Her husband dead, her baby, living perhaps
with an aunt under another name.
Guernica again
hangs before us in the air
as the translators nod and check out
the current slang or a new word
from the war.

The sun is full strength
as I walk out onto Pico.
I take Lydia's testimony home,
stand out on my deck
and look south.

Down the hill, the banana trees
fan each other and two black dogs circle
in a fenced yard.
There are no people on the street
and cars pass like flashes of sun
through the pastel afternoon.

Not here, but somewhere else,
an incident in a field or at a gate
hatches the Guardia like flies.
The interrogation team changes tactics
to machine guns and disappearances.

Not somewhere else, but here,
the poem I am writing
already wonders about its worth.
I won't be shot for what issues
from the small house of my mouth
in this country of the tomb of language.

This poem will never need to lay a finger
to the lips of the person writing it
or head north
wrapped inside a bundle of my clothes.

# In A Little While And The Dog Crying

Horizon the same layers
of melon, lavender, celadon
as yesterday.

An open space blooms in the moment,
rice-paper moon in thin clouds.

In a little while next door
the dog crying
will forget every bit of it.

The bilingual parrot
will be extinguished
for the night.

Momma Kitty hustling early moths
reminds me
it's grown quiet this evening in my heart.

# Wild Mothers

Wild kitty sneaks up my stairs
with two wisps of tiger behind her.
Wild mothers always find me.
Red Tail who lived in my driveway
and that chew-eared thing
who grew old in my carport.
Three bowls of dry food
every day and their tribes
in proscribed circles
waiting for me.
One-legged bluejay, waiting, too.
Lost ocelot hiding in the garage,
escaped cockatoo raucous in the eucalyptus.
Sparrow nesting over my doorway.
Mockingbird in the wisteria.
They find me where the clearing meets
the trees and night and light cross.
I have needed that they weren't mine,
that they would only come that close.

# Payment

French poodles are missing.
Garbage cans get spilled
where condominium tracts
pave over animal trails.
They're setting traps in the foothills
where a coyote carried off a child.
Wilderness not won over creeps back in meaner.

I call it compensation for natural disaster
when flames rise out of Fairfax Avenue
where the city sits on pockets of tar,
when spindly canyon houses and their stilts
wash down after the rains
and mansions explode in the surf at Malibu.

The newly mapped slip-fault
undergirding the high-rise Civic Center testifies
this power will return,
repossessing and collecting its dues.

# This Art, Your Life

The MRI scan reads a tumor in your brain
about the size of an eraser on a pencil,
but what space is it sharing, what room
does it take up, what does it push
aside as it reaches for your optic nerve,
threatening first your color sense, then vision?

I remember you walking to my cabin, a vision
appearing out of nowhere, blowing my brain-
bound sense of rules, operating on nerve
instead, kissing me first, then taking pencil
and paper to sketch the sunlit hills, push
against nightfall and my little room's

lack of light. In bed, there was barely room
to turn over, a small single, but vision
from a larger world was about to push
me past all limits, past what my brain
could handle, our bodies flying, pencil
line strands of hair electric as a nerve

network alight and glowing, each nerve
firing, drawing forth the spirit of the room,
transformed now by our loving. No pencil
sketch, no charcoal smudge, but fiery vision
of what women find and give beyond the brain-
washed fractured ways we've had to push

through to create selves in ourselves, to push
into our books, our paintings—this nerve
of being that shoots straight into the brain,
changing every pathway like arranging room
after room in your house to suit your vision
of space, of light, of how right it was in pencil

drawings. But know each time any pencil
fits into your grip, I wonder as you push
the sketch to fit the scheme of your vision,
are you safe enough? How can I calm you, nervous
as I am, take you into the room
of my heart and keep you from harm? It's brain-

less hoping for such power. Take pencil. Brain-
storm again. Life is what we push for. Make room
for daily dogged vision. Then, live on nerve.

# Into Eternity

*for Pauline*

I fashion a clay boat
for my dog Pauline and me to ride
our souls in.

It's a two seater,
just the two of us into eternity,
riding out the flood of death

like Nuah, the goddess, riding
out her self-generated waters.
She got her name changed to Noah

like the streets downtown
who got their names changed
to English from the Spanish,

the ones who came on boats,
the mixed-blood names cleaned
of mestizo tint or black,

those names that settled
over by the river, over Yagna-na,
the Gabriellino camp.

The new names drive the old
deeper and deeper into the dust,
layering over each other

like the present mind silting over
the geography
of the mind before, forgetting

the first tongue and movement,
the reptile brain and speech of smell.
The new brain stands up on its hind legs
and forgets itself.

But I build a small clay boat
to carry us back to eternity.
Companion species, we will row ourselves
back before our names.

## Other titles from Firebrand Books include:

*Beneath My Heart*, Poetry by Janice Gould/$8.95

*The Big Mama Stories* by Shay Youngblood/$8.95

*A Burst Of Light*, Essays by Audre Lorde/$7.95

*Crime Against Nature*, Poetry by Minnie Bruce Pratt/$8.95

*Diamonds Are A Dyke's Best Friend* by Yvonne Zipter/$9.95

*Dykes To Watch Out For*, Cartoons by Alison Bechdel/$6.95

*Exile In The Promised Land*, A Memoir by Marcia Freedman/$8.95

*Eye Of A Hurricane*, Stories by Ruthann Robson/$8.95

*The Fires Of Bride*, A Novel by Ellen Galford/$8.95

*Food & Spirits*, Stories by Beth Brant/$8.95

*A Gathering Of Spirit*, A Collection by North American Indian Women edited by Beth Brant *(Degonwadonti)*/$9.95

*Getting Home Alive* by Aurora Levins Morales and Rosario Morales /$8.95

*The Gilda Stories*, A Novel by Jewelle Gomez/$9.95

*Good Enough To Eat*, A Novel by Lesléa Newman/$8.95

*Humid Pitch*, Narrative Poetry by Cheryl Clarke/$8.95

*Jewish Women's Call For Peace* edited by Rita Falbel, Irena Klepfisz, and Donna Nevel/$4.95

*Jonestown & Other Madness*, Poetry by Pat Parker/$7.95

*Just Say Yes*, A Novel by Judith McDaniel/$8.95

*The Land Of Look Behind*, Prose and Poetry by Michelle Cliff/$6.95

*A Letter To Harvey Milk*, Short Stories by Lesléa Newman/$8.95

*Letting In The Night*, A Novel by Joan Lindau/$8.95

*Living As A Lesbian*, Poetry by Cheryl Clarke/$7.95

*Making It*, A Woman's Guide to Sex in the Age of AIDS by Cindy Patton and Janis Kelly/$4.95

*Metamorphosis, Reflections On Recovery* by Judith McDaniel/$7.95

*Mohawk Trail* by Beth Brant *(Degonwadonti)*/$7.95

*Moll Cutpurse*, A Novel by Ellen Galford/$7.95

*More Dykes To Watch Out For*, Cartoons by Alison Bechdel/$7.95

*The Monarchs Are Flying*, A Novel by Marion Foster/$8.95

*Movement In Black*, Poetry by Pat Parker/$8.95

*My Mama's Dead Squirrel*, Lesbian Essays on Southern Culture by Mab Segrest/$8.95

*New, Improved! Dykes To Watch Out For,* Cartoons by Alison Bechdel/$7.95

*The Other Sappho,* A Novel by Ellen Frye/$8.95

*Politics Of The Heart,* A Lesbian Parenting Anthology edited by Sandra Pollack and Jeanne Vaughn/$11.95

*Presenting. . . Sister NoBlues* by Hattie Gossett/$8.95

*A Restricted Country* by Joan Nestle/$8.95

*Sacred Space* by Geraldine Hatch Hanon/$9.95

*Sanctuary, A Journey* by Judith McDaniel/$7.95

*Sans Souci,* And Other Stories by Dionne Brand/$8.95

*Scuttlebutt,* A Novel by Jana Williams/$8.95

*Shoulders,* A Novel by Georgia Cotrell/$8.95

*Simple Songs,* Stories by Vickie Sears/$8.95

*The Sun Is Not Merciful,* Short Stories by Anna Lee Walters/$7.95

*Tender Warriors,* A Novel by Rachel Guido deVries/$8.95

*This Is About Incest* by Margaret Randall/$7.95

*The Threshing Floor,* Short Stories by Barbara Burford/$7.95

*Trash,* Stories by Dorothy Allison/$8.95

*The Women Who Hate Me,* Poetry by Dorothy Allison/$8.95

*Words To The Wise,* A Writer's Guide to Feminist and Lesbian Periodicals & Publishers by Andrea Fleck Clardy/$4.95

*Yours In Struggle,* Three Feminist Perspectives on Anti-Semitism and Racism by Elly Bulkin, Minnie Bruce Pratt, and Barbara Smith/$8.95

**You can buy Firebrand titles at your bookstore, or order them directly from the publisher (141 The Commons, Ithaca, New York 14850, 607-272-0000).**

**Please include $2.00 shipping for the first book and $.50 for each additional book.**

**A free catalog is available on request.**